FAIRY TALES

Written by Keith Faulkner
Illustrated by Maureen Galvani

PRICE STERN SLOAN
Los Angeles

Three Little Pigs

Once upon a time there were three little pigs who lived with their mother and father. But as the little pigs grew, the little house they all lived in just wasn't big enough for the whole family any more.

"It's no good," said Father pig. "You three will have to find somewhere else to live."

"I'll build my own house," said the first little pig.

"So will I!" agreed the second little pig.

"Me too!" cried the third little pig.

So, off they went to build their own houses.

The first little pig built himself a house of straw. The second little pig built himself a house of sticks. They had both finished their houses, but the third little pig was still working. He was building a house of bricks. It took a long time to build, but when it was finished, it was warm and cozy inside and very strong indeed.

Just as they had all finished and gone into their houses, there was a knock at the door of the straw house. The little pig peeped out and saw a huge and very hungry-looking wolf at his door.

"Little pig . . . little pig . . . let me in!" said the wolf. But the little pig had locked the door.

"Not by the hair on my chinny-chin-chin. I will not let you in," replied the little pig.

"Then I'll huff and I'll puff and I'll blow your house down."

So, the huge wolf huffed and he puffed and with no trouble at all, he blew the straw house down. Luckily, the little pig escaped and ran to join his brother in the house made of sticks.

A moment later the wolf was knocking on the door of the house made of sticks.

"Little pigs . . . little pigs . . . let me in!" said the wolf. But the little pigs had locked the door.

"Not by the hair on our chinny-chin-chins. We will not let you in," replied the little pigs.

"Then I'll huff and I'll puff and I'll blow your house down."

So, the huge wolf huffed and he puffed and with no trouble at all, he blew the stick house down. The two little pigs ran to join their brother in the house made of bricks.

A moment later the wolf was knocking on the door of the house made of bricks.

"Little pigs . . . little pigs . . . let me in!" said the wolf. But they had locked the door.

"Not by the hair on our chinny-chin-chins. We will not let you in," they replied.

"Then I'll huff and I'll puff and blow your house down."

So, the huge wolf huffed and puffed. Then he huffed and puffed some more, but he could not blow down the house of bricks because it was too strong.

So, the huge hungry wolf climbed up onto the roof. "I'll climb down the chimney and eat you all up," he called down to the three little pigs. But he didn't know that there was a big fire below. Just as he was climbing in the chimney, the fire roared up and burned his tail. OW! The wolf jumped off the roof and ran away, never to be seen again by the three little pigs.

The Princess and the Pea

Long ago, in a faraway land there lived a prince. Although he was handsome and rich, he could not find a princess to marry.

"You can choose any princess," said his mother, the queen. "Surely one of them must be good enough for you, my son."

"Don't worry mother," replied the prince, "I'll search and search until I find a princess to marry."

So, the handsome prince set off in search of a princess. He traveled to many lands, and although he met many princesses, he did not find one whom he wanted to marry.

After years of traveling, he returned home to his father's palace, still without a bride.

One stormy, windswept night, soon after he came home, there was a knock at the palace doors.

"Who could be out on such a night," said the prince to himself, as he pulled the bolt and threw open the great doors. There stood a beautiful young girl. Her long hair was dripping with rain and her clothes were so wet that water was pouring off them.

"Come inside!" cried the prince, as he led her to the roaring fire to warm up.

"You poor girl, what takes you out on such a cold, stormy night. Are you lost?" he asked kindly.

"Yes," she replied sweetly. "My carriage broke down. I am a princess," she explained.

Although the prince was charmed by her beauty, he did not really believe her.

"Perhaps she has heard that I'm looking for a wife and this is all a trick," he thought.

So, the prince spoke to his mother, the queen. The queen went to where the servants were preparing a bed for the girl. She took out a small, dried pea and placed it in the center of the mattress.

"Bring more mattresses. Bring every mattress in the palace," she ordered.

Soon, the pile of mattresses grew and grew, until they almost reached the ceiling. There were twenty-one soft mattresses, and on the bottom one lay the small, dried pea.

The princess was then led to the bed. "I hope you will be comfortable, my dear," said the queen.

In the morning, the princess came down to join the king, queen and prince for breakfast.

"How did you sleep?" inquired the queen.

"I'm afraid I did not sleep well," replied the princess. "I don't want to be rude, but even though there were so many soft mattresses on my bed, I could feel something digging into my back."

"Hoorah!" cried the queen. "Only a true princess would have skin so soft and tender that she would feel a pea through twenty mattresses."

The handsome prince married the princess and the pea was placed in a glass case.

It lies there to this day, to remind people of how their prince met his loving princess.

Rapunzel

Long ago, there lived a good man and his wife in a little house, next door to an evil witch.

While they were expecting their first baby, the woman became so sick that she had to stay in her bed.

"Isn't there anything that will help?" begged the man.

"Bring me some of the herb rapunzel, that grows in the witch's garden," she said.

That night he climbed the wall into the witch's garden.

As he was reaching for the herb, he heard a voice. "Aha! Stealing my herbs, eh!" screeched the witch.

"I need the herb for my wife. If she does not get it, she will die," pleaded the frightened man.

"On one condition," replied the witch. "You must promise to give me your firstborn child!"

The man thought his wife might die, so he agreed.

After she had taken the herb, his wife got better, but when their baby girl was born, the witch came to see them.

"I've come to take the child, as you agreed," she cackled. "I shall call her Rapunzel."

Rapunzel grew into a beautiful girl, with long golden hair, which she wore in a braid.

When she was twelve, the witch locked her in a tall tower in the woods, with no door and only one small window at the very top.

Each day the witch would bring food, stand by the tower and call, "Rapunzel! Rapunzel! Let down your hair." Rapunzel would drop her long braid from the window so that the witch could climb up.

One day a young prince heard Rapunzel's sweet singing. He was listening to her when the witch came again, and he heard her call out to Rapunzel.

So, that evening he went to the foot of the tower and called. "Rapunzel! Rapunzel! Let down your hair." SWISH! Down came Rapunzel's long, golden braid, and he quickly climbed the tower.

"I have come to rescue you," he said to the girl.

"But I cannot climb down my own hair," said Rapunzel. "Bring me silk threads, so I can make a strong rope."

The next time the witch climbed up Rapunzel's hair, the girl spoke without thinking. "Why are you so much heavier than the prince?"

"Aha! You wicked girl," said the witch, as she cut off Rapunzel's long, golden braid. She then took the girl to a lonely valley and left her there.

When the prince came, he called, "Rapunzel! Rapunzel! Let down your hair." But it was the witch who lowered Rapunzel's long braid. The prince began to climb, but the wicked witch let go of the braid and down the prince fell.

The prince fell into the brambles below and was blinded by the sharp thorns. For years he wandered until at last he found his way into the lonely valley.

Suddenly, he heard the sound of a girl's voice singing.

"My sweet Rapunzel!" he cried. As she wept with joy, her tears ran into his eyes and he could see again.

So the prince took Rapunzel back to his kingdom, where they were married.

The Elves and the Shoemaker

"Surely you could work just a little faster, dear," said the shoemaker's wife, as she watched him.

"Oh yes, I could work faster," replied the old shoemaker. "I could cut the leather with less care. I could sew with bigger stitches, but it wouldn't be my best. You know I always like to do my very best."

"Of course you do, but you take such care that we hardly make any money. We only have enough leather for one more pair of shoes," sighed his wife. "Come, it's time for bed."

A little later he went to bed, leaving the cut-out pieces of leather on his bench. Can you imagine his surprise in the morning, when he found the most perfect pair of shoes that he had ever seen?

"Come quickly!" he cried, holding the shoes for his wife to see. "Have you ever seen such tiny stitching?"

They put the shoes into the shop window and they were sold in minutes, for twice the usual price—enough money to buy leather for two more pairs.

That night the shoemaker cut out the leather and left it lying on his bench, just as before. And the next morning, not one, but two pairs of gleaming shoes lay there, as if by magic!

Again the shoes were put into the window and were sold for twice the usual price because the stitching was so fine. Soon, rich people began to hear about the old shoemaker's wonderful shoes.

Every night the shoemaker would cut the leather and leave it on his bench. And every morning the leather had been made into perfect shoes.

One day, the old shoemaker said, "I must find out who is making these shoes for us."

His wife agreed, and that night, after cutting out the leather, they hid and waited.

Then, just as the clock struck twelve, they saw six elves creep from behind the clock. They climbed up onto the bench and began hammering and sewing.

"How cold they look," said the shoemaker's wife.

The next morning the shoemaker's wife cut out some cloth and threaded her needle. She made six tiny pairs of pants and six warm jackets. The old shoemaker made six pairs of tiny boots.

They finished their work just before the clock struck twelve and laid out the little clothes on the bench. As the clock struck, the elves appeared. They were confused when they saw the tiny clothes.

"Hoorah!" The elves jumped with joy, as they tried on their warm, new clothes.

"No more shoemaking for us," they yelled, as they danced off, never to be seen again.

"Oh dear!" sighed the shoemaker's wife. "How will you manage without their help?"

"I shall just do my best," smiled the shoemaker.

Hansel and Gretel

By the edge of a dark forest lived a woodcutter, his children, Hansel and Gretel, and their stepmother, who was cruel and unkind.

"There's not enough food to feed the children," she said to her husband. "Take them into the forest and leave them. They can find food for themselves."

Although the woodcutter argued with his wife, she was so angry that in the end he agreed.

All this time, the children were upstairs listening.

"Don't worry, dear sister, I have a plan," whispered Hansel. So he crept down to the kitchen and stole a piece of bread.

In the morning their wicked stepmother told them. "Hurry children, we are going to the forest with your father."

Into the dark forest they went. But along the way, when no one was looking, Hansel would drop a crumb from his piece of bread.

"You must be tired," said their stepmother. "Rest here and we'll fetch you later."

When the children woke it was dark. Gretel asked Hansel how they could find their way home.

"I used the crumbs from the bread," he explained, but when they looked, there were no crumbs to be seen. They had all been eaten by the birds.

The children slept again, but it was freezing cold. Around them the birds watched. "We ate the crumbs, so we must help them," the birds said.

So they picked up leaves and laid them on the sleeping children, to keep them warm.

In the morning, the children set off to look for their way home. Suddenly, in a clearing in the forest they saw a house made out of good things to eat. The hungry children broke pieces off the house to eat.

"Don't eat my house," said an old woman, who appeared at the door. "Come in and I'll feed you."

But instead of feeding them, she locked Hansel in a cage, because she was really a wicked witch.

"Ha! Ha! I'll fatten you up, my boy. Then I'll cook you for my dinner," she cackled, as she made Gretel scrub and clean her house.

Every day the witch would ask Hansel to poke his finger out through the bars, so she could feel if he was fat enough to eat yet. But the witch could not see very well, so Hansel would hold out a bone.

"No! No! Not fat enough yet," the witch would say. Until one day she said she couldn't wait anymore, and would cook him today.

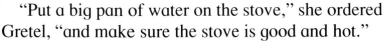

"Put a big pan of water on the stove," she ordered Gretel, "and make sure the stove is good and hot."

Gretel had an idea, and said to the witch, "I'm not sure if the stove is hot enough."

"Oh! Out of my way, stupid girl," snapped the witch, throwing open the stove door and looking in.

In a flash Gretel gave the witch a push. Into the stove she tumbled and was gone! Gretel let her brother out of the cage and they made a sled and piled it high with gingerbread, candy, marshmallow, and all the other food. After a long walk, they found their way home at last.

Their wicked stepmother had run away and their father was feeling very lonely.

Imagine his surprise when he saw them arrive with the sled! They took the food into town and sold it, and made so much money, they never went hungry again!

Sleeping Beauty

The queen cried as she swam in the clear water of the lake.

"Oh, if only I had a child," she sighed. As she did, a tear fell straight into the mouth of a frog, sitting on a lily pad.

"By this time next year, you shall have a daughter," the frog croaked, then it disappeared.

Within a year, the queen had a baby daughter.

"Look, the roses are just beginning to bloom," said the king. "Let's name her Rose. We must not forget to invite the eleven fairies to her christening."

"But, my dear, we only have ten golden plates and the law says that a fairy must only eat from a golden plate," replied the queen.

"Then, only ten fairies will be invited," decided the king." Surely ten is enough."

The day of the christening arrived, and the fairies each brought a gift for the baby.

"My gift is beauty," said the first fairy, touching Rose with her wand. Other fairy gifts were grace, a sweet voice, intelligence, kindness, health, gentleness, happiness, and humor.

But, just as the tenth fairy was about to give her gift, the door burst open and a fairy, all dressed in black, appeared.

It was the eleventh fairy, who had not been invited and she was very angry.

"I will give this child a gift," she cackled. "On her fifteenth birthday, she will prick her finger on the spindle of a spinning wheel and . . . DIE!" With these awful words, the fairy vanished.

"My gift will be that Rose will not die, but sleep, until awoken by the kiss of a true prince," promised the tenth fairy, trying to soften the cursed gift.

Rose grew up beautiful and happy, until the day of her fifteenth birthday party. She and her friends played hide-and-seek around the palace.

Suddenly, Rose found herself alone. Peeping through an open door, she saw an old woman sitting at a spinning wheel.

"Come, help me child," said the old woman. "Here, hold the spindle for me."

As Rose touched the spindle, she felt a pain in her finger.

A moment later every person, from cook to king had fallen sound asleep.

Soon the brambles began to grow around the palace walls and after a hundred years, they were so high and thick that the palace could not be seen.

One day a prince, who had heard the legend of the Sleeping Beauty, came to the overgrown palace.

He drew his sword and hacked through the prickly stems, which seemed to bend before him.

At last, the prince found the beautiful sleeping girl, and he slowly bent to kiss her.

"I have waited so long for you, my prince," she sighed, as she opened her eyes.

Suddenly, everyone in the palace woke up, as if their long sleep had never happened.

Princess Rose and her prince were married and lived happily ever after.

The Gingerbread Man

A little old woman and a little old man lived
together in a little old house. One day the little old
woman was baking. She had made a Gingerbread
Man, with raisin eyes, raisin buttons and a mouth
made from a sliver of orange peel. But, when she
opened the oven door, out jumped the Gingerbread
Man. He ran out of the kitchen and down the lane.
The little old man and the little old woman chased
him, but they could not catch him.

The Gingerbread Man called
over his shoulder to them,
"Run, run as fast as you can,
 You can't catch me,
 I'm the Gingerbread Man!"
Then the Gingerbread Man
passed a cow. "Stop! I'll eat
you up," mooed the cow.
But the Gingerbread Man
just laughed and called out,
"Ha! Ha! I've run away
from a little old woman
and a little old man.
Run, run as fast as you can,
You can't catch me,
I'm the Gingerbread Man!"

Then, the Gingerbread Man passed a horse, as he
ran through the fields.
"Stop! Stop! I'll eat you up," neighed the horse.
But, the Gingerbread Man laughed and called out,
"I've run away from a little old woman, a little
old man, and a cow.
Run, run as fast as you can,
You can't catch me,
I'm the Gingerbread Man!"

As the Gingerbread Man ran toward the river, he saw a fox that was running too.

"I don't want to catch you," said the fox, "I'm being chased by huntsmen myself. Quick, jump on my tail and I'll carry you across the river."

So, the Gingerbread Man jumped on the fox's tail. But as the fox swam across the river he turned to the Gingerbread Man and said, "You're too heavy on my tail, hop onto my back." So, the Gingerbread Man did. A moment later, the fox said, "You'll get wet on my back, climb up onto my shoulder." So, the Gingerbread Man did.

Right in the middle of the river, the fox turned to the Gingerbread Man and said, "I'm sinking! Jump up onto my nose." So, the Gingerbread Man did.

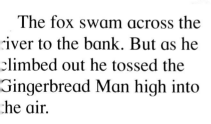

The fox swam across the river to the bank. But as he climbed out he tossed the Gingerbread Man high into the air.

SNAP! Went the fox's jaws.

"Oh, no!" cried the Gingerbread Man, "I'm a quarter gone!"

SNAP! Went the fox's jaws again.

"Oh, no! Now I'm half gone," cried the Gingerbread Man.

SNAP! Went the fox's jaws.

"Mmm! That was yummy," said the fox, licking his lips. The Gingerbread Man said nothing—ever again!

The Ugly Duckling

The mother duck sat on her eggs. Five were small and pale blue, but the sixth was big and white.

Suddenly, the five blue eggs started to hatch. TAP! TAP! CRACK! And out popped five pretty, little, yellow ducklings.

"I suppose that this egg will take longer, because it is the biggest," thought the duck to herself. Then there was a loud CRACK! as the big egg split in two.

It wasn't a pretty, little, yellow duckling, it was a huge, ugly, brown one.

"Oh dear!" quacked the mother duck, "You can't possibly be one of mine!"

The ugly duckling looked very sad and tried to hide with its brothers and sisters.

"You're not one of us!" they said, as they began to laugh.

Then the father duck came to see his new ducklings. The ugly duckling waddled up, flapping his little wings.

"What is that? Not one of ours, I hope," quacked the father duck, turning away.

Then, the hens from the farmyard came over to look at the new ducklings.

"I think it's a baby turkey," laughed one of the hens, seeing the ugly duckling. "It's so ugly."

"It is not a turkey," quacked the mother duck. "Look, I'll show you," and she led her ducklings down to the water. All the ducklings dived in and paddled along behind her, but the ugly duckling could swim even better than his brothers and sisters.

Even the farmer's children came to look. How they laughed at the ugly duckling.

The ugly duckling was very sad and a big tear trickled down his beak. Looking up he saw a flock of white swans, flying away for the winter.

Later that day the farmer's children came back.

"Look! There's that ugly duckling again," they shouted. "He's really a goose. Let's catch him and take him home."

The ugly duckling heard them and paddled deep into the reeds to hide.

All through the winter, the ugly duckling hid in the reeds, cold and lonely. But spring came at last and the weather grew warmer.

Once again, the ugly duckling looked up to see the flock of swans returning to the river.

They landed in the water nearby and one of them sailed gracefully toward him.

"Oh dear! They're going to send me away," thought the ugly duckling.

But, the swan spoke, "Why is a splendid swan like you all alone?" the swan said.

"Me? A swan?" gasped the ugly duckling.

"Yes, of course. Look into the water and you'll see," replied the swan.

So, the ugly duckling gazed into the still water and saw that he was now a beautiful white swan, with the longest and most graceful neck that anyone had ever seen!

Jack and the Beanstalk

Once upon a time, there was a poor widow who had a son called Jack. They had one cow that was too old to give any milk, so the widow decided to sell it.

"Take the cow to sell at the market, Jack," she said. Along the way, he met a strange little man.

"Give me the cow and I will give you these magic beans," said the little man.

Jack ran home to his mother. "Look mother! Magic beans for our old cow," he cried. But his mother was very angry, and threw them out of the window. The next morning, Jack saw a gigantic beanstalk. He shouted good-bye to his mother and then began to climb.

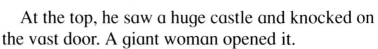

At the top, he saw a huge castle and knocked on the vast door. A giant woman opened it.

"And what do you want?" she asked.

"Could I have something to eat?" asked Jack.

"No! You have to go!" replied the woman. "My husband will be home soon and he eats little boys like you." But, just at that moment, she heard her husband coming back. "Quick! Hide in the oven," she said. Just as Jack scrambled into the oven, the giant burst into the kitchen and sniffed the air . . .

"Fee, fi, fo, fum, I smell the blood of an Englishman."

"No, no, no, dear. I think you're wrong. Sit down and have some food," said his wife.

After eating, the giant called for his magic hen. His wife brought him the hen and Jack peeped from the oven and saw it lay a golden egg.

Soon the giant was asleep and Jack grabbed the hen and ran back to the beanstalk.

With a magic hen to lay golden eggs, Jack and his mother were rich at last.

But Jack wanted to go back up the beanstalk. This time he didn't knock at the door, but crept in and hid in a bucket. While Jack was hiding, the giant came home. He stopped and sniffed the air.

"AHA! Is that thief back again?" he bellowed.

"Well, if that little thief is here, he'll be hiding in the oven," said the giant's wife.

The giant opened the oven door, but Jack wasn't there. After the giant had eaten his meal, he called for his magic harp that played all by itself.

At last, the giant fell asleep and out Jack crept. But, just as Jack snatched the harp, it began to shout. "HELP! HELP!"

The giant woke and chased Jack to the beanstalk. Down Jack climbed, as fast as he could but the giant was close behind him.

"Quick, Mother! Bring the axe," he yelled. Jack began to chop at the thick beanstalk. CHOP! CHOP! Suddenly, it began to groan, then with an enormous THUD! the beanstalk and the giant came crashing down.

So, with the hen that laid golden eggs and the harp that played beautiful music, Jack and his mother lived happily for the rest of their days.

Little Red Riding Hood

"Grandmother is very ill," said Little Red Riding Hood's mother. "Take this basket of food to her."

"Now, be careful in the woods and remember not to talk to strangers," her mother warned.

So, Red Riding Hood set off through the woods to her Grandmother's cottage. She was skipping along when she saw someone by the path.

"Where are you going, Little Red Riding Hood?" the stranger asked in a gruff voice.

"I am taking some food to my sick Grandmother," she explained.

"Don't you think that your Grandmother would like some flowers too?" suggested the stranger, as he stooped to pick some wildflowers.

"Oh! Thank you. You are very nice," replied Red Riding Hood, putting the flowers into her basket.

She said good-bye to the kind stranger and set off on her way.

She didn't know that the wolf, for that is what the stranger was, had raced ahead to her Grandmother's cottage and was knocking on the door.

"Grandmother! It is I, Red Riding Hood," called the wolf, in a little girl's voice.

"Lift the latch and come in, my dear," replied Grandmother.

The wolf leaped in, rushed into the Grandmother's room and gobbled her up in one GULP